The Soul's Touch

A Quiet Journey Into Awakening And Healing

Dr Faris Basheer Mohamed

ISBN: 978-93-343-0821-1

Published by: Blue Loom Books

Contents

Dedication

To the one holding this book—

If you've ever felt like you didn't belong,

or like you were too much for this world,

know that these pages were written for you.

May this story remind you

that sensitivity is a quiet kind of strength.

That love—soft, steadfast—can still move mountains.

And that your soul always knows the way home,

even when your mind has forgotten the map.

Thank you for finding this story—

or perhaps, for letting it find you.

Prologue
The Descent

Before breath, before blood and memory—

Kael danced with the stars.

He was not born, but sent.

In the upper realms, where thought and feeling were one,

and the stars pulsed like heartbeats made of music,

Kael moved through constellations like a song carried on light.

He could see the threads of fate—

golden filaments weaving lives and moments into a vast, living design.

He sang them sometimes, and the threads shimmered in reply.

He was a Flame bearer—

keeper of truth, silent watcher of the unfolding whole,
guardian of harmony.

In that place, truth was untouched—perfect and eternal.

The air tasted of light. Every breath hummed with purpose.

But Kael wondered, as no one else did:

Why is it so hard to carry something so true?

The moment his question left him, the stars hushed.

The golden threads stilled.

They trembled—as if holding their breath.

And then the Voice came—

not as thunder. Not even sound.

It moved through the stillness like light through water—

not commanding, but inviting.

"You must descend," it said.

"Carry the flame where it is needed most."

"To conquer?" Kael asked.

"No. To feel."

"To teach?"

"To live—where truth is hardest to remember."

Kael hesitated.

He had seen the worlds below.

He had glimpsed the suffering—

the broken promises,

the long silences at dinner tables,

the children weeping behind closed doors,

the way beauty sparked and faded into routine.

He knew truth still pulsed beneath it all—bright, unbroken.

And yet, they turned from it.

"Why do they fear the very thing that could heal them?" he asked.

"Why look away from what is already burning inside them?"

The Voice whispered:

"Because truth asks everything.

In the forgetting, you will remember.

In the resistance, you will learn how to love.

Let it burn through you—

and you will understand."

Kael turned to the tapestry one last time.

The threads shimmered, uncertain now—some dimmed, some torn.

A single one—glowing like an ember—fluttered like a flame in wind.

It pulsed with something fragile. Something unfinished.

His thread.

He looked at it and knew: it was waiting for him.

A life not yet lived.

A burden. A hope.

A promise stitched into breath.

Around him, the stars began to recede.

The constellations that once sang to him fell silent.

Light thinned, as if the very fabric of being was folding inward.

A hush—deeper than silence—pressed against him.

Not cold, but vast.

He passed through the veil.

And so—he fell.

He did not crash into matter as a comet, nor split the sky with fire.

He was born as a breath, in silence,

in the quiet corner of an ordinary hospital bed—

the kind the world overlooks,

but cradled in the same holy hush that surrounds all things,

where the Divine whispers creation into being:

His mother clutched him with trembling hands.

She had no partner, no money, and no certainty—

only a quiet strength,

and eyes that somehow recognized him.

"Kael," she whispered.

"You feel like a second chance."

He cried softly.

Not from pain—

but from the weight of forgetting.

The ache of light dimming inside him.

The stars were gone.

The threads were hidden.

But warmth flickered from the ember that endured,

buried deep in the quiet of his heart—

a warmth he couldn't name,

but that would one day rise,

asking to be remembered.

Chapter 1

The Quiet Ache

Kael was a quiet child.

Not shy.

Not fearful.

Just quiet in a way that felt older than the room around him.

He didn't cry loudly.

Didn't scream for attention.

His gray-blue eyes were always searching,

as if asking questions no one else could hear.

He noticed things others didn't—

the way his mother's smile tightened when she opened the mailbox,

how Mr. Harrow, their neighbor, stared at the floor too long when someone mentioned his late wife, the tremble in a teacher's voice when she said, "Everything's fine."

Kael noticed the loneliness behind the laughter.

The ache beneath the silence.

But he didn't have words for it.

Only feelings.

So many feelings.

When he cried in class after the teacher shouted at a boy who hadn't done anything wrong, the others laughed.

When he brought a bird with a broken wing to school, a girl wrinkled her nose and called him "weird."

By the time he was seven, he had already begun tucking them away.

Folding them small.

Hiding them deep.

At home, his mother loved him. He felt it.

She worked long shifts at the metalworks factory—

her hands always smelled faintly of iron and soap.

When she came home, her shoulders sagged under invisible weight.

But still, she cooked.

Still, she folded laundry.

Still, she kissed the top of Kael's head as she passed him on the way to bed.

They didn't talk much—not deeply.

She didn't always know how to ask what he needed.

And Kael didn't know how to answer what she never said.

But sometimes—when the world was quiet and she had a little breath left—

she would sit on the edge of his bed, run her fingers through his hair, and whisper:

> "You've always felt too much, baby.
>
> I don't always know what to do with that.
>
> But I love you. I swear, I do."

Kael didn't always understand.

But he held her voice in his chest like a warm stone.

It wasn't a language he could build his soul on—

but it was something.

It was enough to keep him tethered.

Until one day, it wasn't.

There was an ache in Kael that had no name.

Not a hunger for food.

Not a longing for toys or friends.

Something else.

A homesickness for a place he'd never seen.

A memory he didn't have.

At night, he would sit by the window while his mother made dinner,

watching dusk settle like a secret.

He stared at the passing headlights like brief visitors from another world.

He didn't know what he was waiting for.

Only that he was.

When he turned seven, he had a dream.

He was floating above a garden of stars.

The sky wasn't empty—it was woven like cloth.

Strands of gold, light, and breath moved through everything.

And Kael—without hands or voice—reached for it.

Not to touch it.

But to belong to it.

When he woke, his face was wet with tears.

He didn't know why.

His mother found him at the kitchen table before dawn, clutching a piece of paper.

It wasn't a drawing. Not really.

Just strands and swirls and something that looked like a thread trying to remember itself.

She brushed his hair back and sat beside him.

"Bad dream?" she asked.

Kael shook his head.

"Not bad," he whispered.

"Just... gone."

She didn't understand.

But she made him toast.

And sat with him in the hush.

At school, he learned how to blend in.

To smile when others smiled.

To speak just enough.

To stop asking strange questions.

To stop crying when he saw someone eating alone.

But some part of him always stayed watching.

Feeling.

Waiting.

One day, a girl in his class had tears in her eyes but was laughing anyway.

Everyone else believed the laugh.

Kael didn't.

He looked at her.

Saw the tears she tried to blink away.

He didn't say anything.

Just sat beside her after class.

They didn't speak.

But after a while, she looked at him and said:

"Thanks."

He didn't know what for.

But something in him stirred.

That night, the ember glowed for the first time.

Not as light.

Not as vision.

Just a warmth.

A stillness deep in his chest—

like something inside him had recognized itself.

He didn't know what it was.

Only that it mattered.

His mother didn't always understand his quiet.

She didn't always know how to meet the deep places in him.

But in her hands, there was warmth.

And in her trying, there was love.

And though Kael had no name for what he was becoming,

the longing inside him had begun to burn—

not as fire,

but as a small ache that felt like a memory.

And when the ache grew too loud, Kael sometimes wandered.

Not to find anything—

just to breathe where the sky felt wider.

Once, as he sat on a hill above the streetlights, he thought he heard a sound—

a soft humming, like breath woven into wind.

He turned his head, but nothing was there.

Still, the warmth in his chest answered.

He didn't tell anyone. But he began to listen.

Chapter 2
The Garden Door

Kael was around ten or eleven when he found the garden.

It wasn't planned.

He'd wandered too far from the library one afternoon, down a street that didn't feel familiar—but didn't feel unfamiliar either.

A cracked gate.

Overgrown vines.

A low wall stained with moss.

The scent of lavender and mint hanging thick in the warm air.

The gate opened at his touch with a long, aching sigh.

Inside:

Crooked stepping stones.

Wild herbs spilling from raised beds.

A wind chime turning gently, though the air was still.

And there—kneeling in the dirt—an old woman, humming.

She didn't look up when he entered.

Only when he stepped closer did her voice rise—weathered but kind.

"You have quiet feet," *she said.*

"Most people stomp through the world like they're trying to prove they exist."

He said nothing. But something in him slowed.

Settled.

Rosemary filled her hands, earth clinging like it trusted her touch.

She still hadn't looked at him.

"Want to help?" she asked.

He hesitated. Shrugged.

"No pressure," she added. *"The ground only grows what's given freely."*

That sentence landed somewhere deeper than it should have.

He knelt beside her.

She handed him a trowel.

They worked in silence.

Not the kind of silence that feels awkward or empty.

The kind that feels held.

Her name didn't come that day.

But he came back the next.

And the next.

Not every day.

But often enough that she started saving him a second pair of gloves on the ledge.

Eventually, he learned her name was Mira.

But by then, he already knew what she was:

Safe.

There were no questions he couldn't answer.

No lessons, no corrections.

Just space to be.

And somehow, in that letting—he felt more real.

One afternoon, as they pruned back a rosemary bush that had grown wild around the fence, Mira said:

"You see more than you say."

Kael looked up.

"That's not a flaw," she added. "It's a kind of flame. Not everyone burns loud."

He didn't know why, but his throat caught.

She said nothing more. Just kept pruning.

He began noticing more—not just in the garden, but in himself.

When someone cried quietly on the bus and hid it behind a windowpane, he didn't look away.

When his mother came home exhausted and said she was "fine," he heard the wear in her bones.

When a teacher snapped and then sat too still, Kael saw the tremble in his hands.

And somewhere inside him, Mira's words echoed:

It's a kind of flame.

Kael sometimes wondered who had come before him—

drawn by the same quiet, the same earth.

Mira never said.

But the garden remembered.

In tools worn smooth by other hands.

In pathways softened by familiar steps.

In blossoms that felt like echoes.

Others came.

Not often.

Not loudly.

An older man once left a basket of apricots at the gate, as if in thanks.

A woman tended the sunflowers for a season—never speaking, just weeding gently, then vanishing like mist.

A girl with too many bracelets trimmed vines for a few weeks and disappeared between one spring and the next.

They never stayed long.

But they came.

And Kael noticed—

they never spoke to Mira while he was there.

They came quietly, moved softly,

and left without needing to be seen.

As if they understood:

The flame doesn't bloom beneath a crowd.

As if they remembered:

Some moments aren't shared. They're witnessed.

Mira didn't call them.

She didn't need to.

They were guided.

Like he had been.

It took Kael a while to understand this was her way—

Not chasing.

Not correcting.

Just tending what arrives with care.

"*Some flames,*" Mira had once said, "*grow best when still.*"

One day, Kael brought her a seedling he had tried to grow at home.

It was lopsided, clumsy, barely alive.

Mira held it in both hands like it was sacred.

"Plants grow toward whatever light they can find," she said softly.

He didn't know if she meant the plant.

Or him.

Maybe both.

Sometimes they planted things.

Sometimes they just sat.

Sometimes Mira told stories—not fairy tales, but strange, shimmering truths.

Of souls who traveled between worlds.

Of fire hidden in bones.

Of angels who wore no wings, only presence.

Once, she tucked a mint sprig into his palm.

"This," she said, "is what trust smells like."

He didn't understand.

But he smiled anyway.

“*You’ve felt too much, haven’t you*?” she asked one golden afternoon.

Kael nodded.

“*The world doesn’t know what to do with hearts like yours.*” she said.

“*So it tries to make you forget.*”

“*Is it bad?*” he asked. “*To feel too much?*”

She chuckled—like wind stirring dry leaves.

“*Not bad. Just rare. Most people protect themselves from feeling. But you—your soul came here with its doors wide open.*”

Kael blinked at her.

“How do you know?”

She picked a fallen flower and placed it in his hand.

“Because you came to my gate,” she said.

“The ones with open hearts always do.”

They sat beneath the olive tree as the sun shifted through the leaves.

Kael didn’t speak.

He didn’t need to.

Something in him was loosening.

Unclenching.

And though he didn't have a word for it yet,

He knew he would return.

Not just to the garden.

But to himself.

Chapter 3

The Edge of Things

Kael was thirteen when the world began to grow louder around him.

Not in volume—but in conflict.

Peers tested boundaries.

Teachers stretched expectations.

The air buzzed with tension, competition, and hollow bravado.

Kael didn't push back. He pulled inward.

He drifted from conversations, stared out of windows, and scribbled questions in the margins of worksheets that didn't ask anything real.

Not because he was bored, but because most of what people said didn't seem to say anything at all.

He wasn't lonely.

But he was often alone.

Mira remained his quiet center.

By now, Kael tended the garden like it was part of him. He knew when the mint needed thinning, when to let the dill bolt, how to sense the soil's mood just by smell.

He spoke more around her. Still not much—but enough. She never rushed him.

"Some truths grow slowly," she once said, lifting a stubborn root with delicate hands. "Like roots underground. If you dig too fast, you kill them."

Still, the world outside the garden was relentless. Louder in its demands. Sharper in its judgments. More insistent in asking him to become something else.

His classmates laughed at the way he moved through thoughts like weather. Teachers called him bright—but distant. Even his mother—still loving, still trying—had begun to say things like,

"You need to toughen up."

"The world won't hold your hand forever."

"You can't let everything get to you."

The moment those words fell from his mother's mouth, Kael felt them hit him, like a stone sinking into soft earth. How could he separate the world's weight from the weight he carried inside?

The world won't hold your hand forever.

No, it wouldn't. He had already felt that. But what if letting go—what if not holding onto things—was what would leave him hollow?

But Kael didn't know how not to let it in. He felt it all.

The loneliness behind a classmate's bragging.

The flinch in a girl's eyes when her name was called.

The weariness in a teacher's voice when she spoke of deadlines and "growing up."

It all moved through him like wind through open windows. Though he didn't want to close those windows, he feared he'd drown in what they let in.

So, he began to shift.

Not with rebellion. Not in defiance. But in small, practiced quietings.

He stopped writing poems in the margins of his notes.

Stopped asking questions with no clear answers.

Stopped visiting the garden as often.

Not because he didn't want to—but because he feared Mira would see how far he'd already drifted from himself.

He tried to be what the world applauded:

Faster.

Firmer.

Less strange.

Less soft.

But the more he dimmed, the hollower he felt. At first, it was just a weariness in his chest, a quiet ache behind his eyes. But soon, it became something he couldn't ignore.

It happened in a hallway, between classes.

Lockers slammed shut like gunshots.

Jovi—a quiet boy, always alone—was shoved into a locker by two others.

It wasn't the first time.

Kael saw.

Jovi looked up—face flushed, jaw set, trying not to care.

Their eyes met.

Just for a moment. Not a plea. Just a knowing.

And Kael looked away. He felt the heat rise in his chest—the flicker of the flame, asking him to move, to speak. But he didn't. He kept walking.

And something inside him cracked. Not because of what he'd done—but because of what he hadn't.

Later that week, Kael found himself back at Mira's Garden. The wind was sharp. The sky clouded.

He didn't say a word for a long time.

Mira, who had always respected silence, spoke.

"Tell me what you didn't do."

Kael's throat tightened.

"I didn't help him."

"Why not?"

He stared at the dirt.

"Because I didn't want to be him."

Mira was quiet.

Kael's voice cracked.

"It's easier to hide. It hurts too much to feel everything. It makes me weak."

"No," she said softly. "It makes you awake."

"But it doesn't help anyone," he said. "And it's tearing me apart."

She reached out and took his hand.

"You didn't do nothing. You felt it. You broke a little. That means you're still here."

He didn't respond. But her gaze held him—steady, gentle, vast.

"This world is heavy, Kael. The more open your heart, the more weight you feel. But don't mistake sensitivity for failure. The ones who feel most deeply are not weak. They're just holding more."

Kael closed his eyes.

"Then why does it feel like I'm falling apart?"

"Because something false is falling away—the walls you built to protect yourself."

She let the words settle.

Then:

"You can numb yourself, if you want.

You can play the part.

Most people do.

But the cost is high.

You lose the very thing that makes you light."

He looked at her, eyes brimming.

"I don't know if I can carry it."

"You're not meant to carry it all," she said.

"Just the part that is yours. The part that says, I will not abandon my heart to survive."

That night, Kael didn't make any grand vows. He didn't suddenly return to who he had been. But he did cry. Not for Jovi. Not for Mira. For himself. For the part of him that had almost disappeared.

And somewhere inside him, the flame flickered. Dimmed. But did not go out.

And though he didn't yet know, what flickered in him would stir quiet embers in others.

Chapter 4
Where Roots Find Stone

Later that year, Mira quietly mentioned a youth co-op that needed volunteers.

"You're ready," she said.

Not as advice.

As a knowing.

Kael didn't know what he'd be asked to do—only that it mattered. That it was time to begin giving back the warmth he'd learned to hold.

The next day, he walked through the side door of the co-op.

It smelled like overripe tomatoes and floor cleaner.

Mismatched shelves and hand-scrawled signs made it feel more like a garage that had opened its heart—a place that didn't try to impress you, only hold you.

Like a garden that never bloomed all at once, but still grew something real.

A woman handed him a name tag without looking up.

"New volunteer?"

He nodded.

She gestured. "Soren will show you what's what."

Soren didn't look up.

"Grab gloves," he said, tossing a box toward compost bags.

"If you've got a clean shirt by the end of the day, you did it wrong."

He was loud without shouting. Sharp-eyed. Sleeves always rolled, like he was ready to fix something or break it. Older than Kael. Practical. Sarcastic.

Not unkind—but allergic to silence, softness, and slowness.

Which meant—he didn't like Kael.

Not at first.

"You meditate or something?" Soren asked one morning.

"You've got that monk face. Like you're here, but not really."

Kael didn't answer.

Soren muttered, "Weird thing is... people listen to you anyway."

Kael started volunteering Saturdays.

Organizing shelves. Repotting herbs. Listening.

The quiet rhythm of work spoke louder than words.

Weeks blurred together—soil, silence, small rituals.

Then one afternoon, she arrived.

Niva.

A friend of someone on the community board.

She showed up with a sketchbook under one arm and ink smudges on her fingers.

Not polished. Not practiced.

More like a candle determined not to go out.

"Hi!" she said, catching Kael mid-shelf. "I figured plants don't judge."

She smiled. "You don't talk much, huh?"

Kael shook his head—not as an answer, more as acknowledgment.

"Cool," she said. "Talking too much gets you into trouble."

Soren raised an eyebrow later.

"Floaty," he muttered. "Like someone who thinks good vibes can fix a leaking roof."

Kael noticed Niva had heard.

She said nothing.

But the next day, she brought a screwdriver and quietly fixed a shelf.

The three of them—Kael, Niva, and Soren—began to orbit each other.

Not as friends. Not yet.

But as presences.

Kael observed.

Niva reached.

Soren resisted.

And still—something grew.

Like roots pressing against stone.

Somewhere in those afternoons, Kael began keeping a notebook.

He called it The Book of Flamekeepers.

He didn't know why it mattered.

Only that it did.

He wrote names like a prayer—

Soren — armor over ache

Niva — afraid of fading out

No stories. Just truths.

One weekend, the co-op partnered with the library for a donation sort.

Kael and Soren were sent to help.

That's where Kael saw him—

A boy, thirteen maybe, stacking books by a cart.

Arms wobbling under the weight.

A supervisor hovered nearby—impatient. Constant.

"Not like that. Faster. Again."

Kael stood sorting a tray of cracked-spine poetry.

He felt the boy shrink.

Felt the flame flicker.

He wanted to believe presence was enough.

That standing near could soften the moment.

It didn't.

The boy's hands fumbled. His shoulders curled.

Then Soren stepped in.

"Hey. He's a kid. Not a machine. Back off."

The supervisor blinked. Stepped away.

Soren knelt beside the boy and helped restack the books.

No commentary. Just quiet action.

Kael watched.

And something stirred—not guilt, but clarity.

Later, he sat beside Mira in the garden.

"I felt it rise in me," he told her. "But I held back.

I thought presence could speak for me.

But it didn't. Soren did."

Mira said nothing at first.

Then she looked up, eyes steady.

"Then speak," she said.

"The flame doesn't ask you to be passive. It asks you to be true."

Kael stiffened—startled by the fire in her calm.

"Sometimes truth whispers," she said.

"But sometimes it thunders.

Not to shame—but to interrupt harm.

Not to control—but to protect what is sacred."

She reached for his hand.

"Use gentleness when strength is needed—and you betray the flame.

Use force when tenderness is called for—and you do the same."

Her grip was light. Her voice, steel.

"You must learn to burn in both directions—

with softness and with steel.

That is what it means to carry the flame."

Kael didn't answer.

But something in him shifted.

Not broken. Not burned.

Just… changed.

So the next time he returned—

he didn't come carrying only stillness.

He came with clarity.

And the quiet courage to speak.

Chapter 5

The Ones Yet to Wake

Kael often sat with those in pain—silent, asking nothing. Even when they turned away, he stayed.

He met them often—those who scoffed at kindness.

Men and women who wore anger like armor.

Children already fluent in the language of distrust.

Elders who had outlived too much joy to trust anything gentle.

Some turned their backs before he even approached.

Some mocked the gentleness they didn't understand.

One man spat at Kael in a market, calling him "a fool with soft eyes."

Another laughed when Kael paused to honor a stranger who had died.

"What's the use of grieving someone you never knew?" the man snapped.

Not everyone wanted what Kael carried.

Some had been burned so many times that even mercy felt threatening.

One morning, outside the co-op, Kael met a man—loud, angry, unmoved.

"You think standing still and listening makes a difference?" the man barked.

"People like you burn out first." Kael didn't argue.

He never fought back—not because he lacked words, but because he carried different ones.

"You think you're better?" the man demanded.

"No," Kael said softly.

"I think I'm still learning."

The man rolled his eyes and walked away.

Kael carried the moment with him.

It echoed others he had known…

There were many like him—Darion, the man in the coffee shop.

Sharp suit. Cold eyes. Every word calculated.

"You one of those kind-hearted types?" Darion had asked, a smirk in his voice.

"People like you get eaten out here."

Kael had only smiled.

"People like me don't stop being people," he answered.

Darion laughed—dry, brittle.

"Good luck with that."

He turned to go.

But before he left, he said gently:

"Kindness isn't weakness. It's just painful to relearn."

Darion didn't respond.

But he watched Kael go.

And sometimes, Kael had learned, a glance was enough.
For now.

That night, sleep did not come easily. The man's words lingered like smoke, bitter in Kael's lungs.

When dawn painted the fog silver, he returned to the garden.

Mist clung to the ground, soft as breath, blurring its edges.

Above, the stars were veiled by drifting clouds.

Mira sat beneath the olive tree, weaving dried sage into little bundles.

She didn't look up when he arrived.

She didn't need to.

Kael sat beside her.

The questions rose in him like scent from wet earth.

"What about the ones who never listen?" he asked.

"The ones who hurt others and never come back?

The ones who leave behind silence without apology?"

Mira stirred the bundle in her lap, her hands moving like memory.

"The flame never forces," she said.

"It only offers."

"If they turn away, it doesn't burn them," she continued, voice calm.

"It simply waits.

Not with judgment.

With mercy.

It warms the edges.

It makes room."

Kael looked down at his hands.

"Are there those who go untouched?"

Mira nodded slowly.

"Some pass-through life untouched by the flame.

Not because it wasn't there—

but because they were too afraid to feel."

Kael's heart ached—not with anger, but with a sorrow that stretched deeper than words.

"Do they ever come back?" he whispered.

Kael swallowed, unsure whether he wanted the answer to be yes—or no.

Part of him ached to believe in return. Another part feared the silence.

Mira's gaze softened even further.

"Not always."

Mira paused—a breath held between sorrow and hope.

"But sometimes… they return.

Not as the same soul—

but the same ache, the same question, woven into another life.

Another story.

Another chance.

She leaned back against the old stone, watching a crow glide low across the gray sky.

"Love doesn't erase what's been done, Kael.

But it holds the thread—

waiting for the moment someone is ready to stitch it forward."

They sat in silence, the mist settling around them like a soft veil.

Mira's voice dropped lower, nearly disappearing into the evening:

"No light is wasted.

Even if it doesn't reach the one it first called to."

Kael let her words settle, feeling the ache of it stretch through his chest.

And somewhere deep inside, he began to understand:

Justice wasn't only about punishment.

It wasn't about who deserved what.

Justice is the quiet, relentless offering of light—

again and again—

"Until every soul must choose—to open, or to stay closed."

Kael closed his eyes.

He didn't know if the man by the bridge would ever soften.

Or the one in the market.

Or Darion, with his hollow laugh that never quite reached his eyes.

But he knew this:

The flame doesn't stop offering.

It simply moves to where it's welcomed.

Some souls die with unopened hearts.

Their threads are not cut from the tapestry.

They remain—silent. Unlit.

Held in the quiet beyond choice.

In his notebook that night, Kael wrote:

Some doors stay closed for lifetimes—

The flame knocks anyway.

Somewhere in the distance, a single flame flickered in a window.

It was enough.

It was always enough.

Chapter 6
Trust the Reaching

Niva started talking faster around Kael after a few weeks.

Not with purpose.

Just with effort—like someone swimming harder because they'd never learned to float.

She talked about anything—funny signs, awkward customers, stubborn tomato plants forcing their way through the alley cracks behind the co-op.

Kael didn't interrupt.

He didn't encourage, either.

He just listened—steady, present, unhurried.

It should have calmed her.

But somehow, it made the silence between them feel heavier.

Not awkward. Just… honest.

And honesty, Niva was learning, had weight.

She fidgeted more.

Dropped things more.

Bit her lip between thoughts and laughed too loudly at her own jokes.

One afternoon, while they were stacking seed trays near the back window, it cracked.

She set down a tray with a sharper clatter than necessary and blurted:

"You make me feel like I'm too much and not enough at the same time, you know that?"

The words fell between them—raw, unpolished.

Kael looked up, startled.

Before he could find a response, Soren—pretending to sort tools across the room—snorted.

"Welcome to planet Earth," he muttered, tossing a wrench into the bin harder than necessary.

Niva flushed, tugging at the loose threads on her sleeves.

Kael opened his mouth—then closed it again.

Because he didn't know how to explain the truth sitting quietly in his chest:

That he hadn't meant to make her feel small.

That he saw her brightness—not as a flaw, but as proof she hadn't given up.

That he liked her exactly as she was.

Even when she didn't know how to be still.

But some truths can't be spoken all at once.

Some truths have to breathe first.

So instead, Kael set down his tray more gently this time.

And let the silence between them say what words could not:

I see you. You don't have to fill the space to be welcome here.

Across the room, Soren didn't say anything else.

But his gaze lingered longer than usual, something unreadable flickering behind the usual sarcasm—

as if part of him wanted to protect Niva from the world's sharpness,

and part of him didn't know how.

They went back to work.

Three points on the same uncertain wheel.

Turning toward something none of them could name yet.

Already—unseen—the roots were pressing forward.

Through stone.

Through fear.

Toward a light they hadn't yet learned how to trust.

Niva didn't say goodbye.

She just wasn't there one Saturday.

Kael noticed it first—the untouched tray of herbs.

Then the empty chair she always dragged closer to the window.

The co-op hummed around him like usual—voices, footsteps, the scrape of crates—

but something inside him tilted.

When he asked the woman with the clipboard, she only shrugged.

"Said she needed time. Didn't leave details."

It wasn't like Niva to leave without a word.

Except—maybe it was.

The way a candle sputters before going out.

Later that afternoon, as Kael organized seed packets, he found it.

A folded piece of paper, tucked behind the basil sprigs.

No name on the outside.

But he knew.

Inside, a few uneven lines in Niva's looping handwriting:

It's not your fault.

It's just... things got stirred up, and I don't know where to put them yet.

Thanks for not looking away.

Kael stood there a long time, the note fluttering slightly in the breeze from the broken ceiling fan.

He didn't cry.

He didn't chase.

He just let the ache move through him the way Mira had taught him—

like weather through trees, without fighting it.

Deep inside, something tightened.

Some losses didn't shout.

They whispered.

Soren noticed, of course.

He came over, tossing a bag of potting soil onto the shelf—louder than necessary, but not angry.

Almost careful.

“You look like someone lost a pet,” he said, voice gruff.

Kael didn’t answer.

Soren scratched the back of his neck, then muttered,

“People leave, monk-boy.

She’ll be fine. Probably yelling at the moon somewhere.”

No lecture.

No big brotherly wisdom.

Just that.

Kael tucked Niva’s note into the back of his notebook—the one he saved for names, for moments, for remembering.

He didn’t write anything new that day.

Some goodbyes didn’t need to be named.

Only honored.

Later that week, Kael found himself back at the garden.

The sky was pale and heavy, rosemary brushing against his hands as he passed.

Mira sat on the stone bench, needle in hand, slowly mending a frayed edge of cloth.

Beside her, Kael settled into the breathing quiet, and for a long while, neither of them said a word.

Finally, Kael spoke:

"I think… I hurt someone. Without meaning to."

Mira drew the needle through one more stitch before answering.

"Presence," she said softly, "doesn't always soothe, Kael.

Sometimes it stirs."

Kael frowned.

"But I didn't do anything."

She smiled—a sad, knowing smile.

"That's why."

She folded the cloth gently and set it beside her, then met his gaze.

"When you stay still enough, you become a mirror.

And not everyone is ready to see what's reflected."

Kael twisted a fallen leaf between his fingers.

"I didn't want her to feel small."

Mira's voice remained gentle, but sure:

"You didn't make her small.

You revealed where she already felt small."

She brushed a stray thread from her lap.

"Kindness isn't about comfort all the time.

It's about staying—especially when the truth gets hard to hold."

Kael swallowed.

Stillness settled over the garden, soft and close, as if the world were holding its breath.

"Will she be okay?" he asked.

Mira leaned back, watching a crow drift across the gray sky.

"Roots find stone," she murmured.

"But they also find ways through."

She turned back to him, her voice barely above a whisper:

"Trust the reaching."

Kael didn't answer.

He just sat there, letting the stillness, the ache, and the hope settle into him,

quiet as new roots threading through the cracks in stone.

Chapter 7

After the Words

The community gathering was held in the hall next to the old library.

Twinkle lights dangled from the rafters. Lavender lay scattered at the doorway, like an afterthought. The room smelled faintly of incense and printer ink—as if someone had tried to smudge serenity over paperwork.

Cushions were arranged in careful circles. Crystals gleamed in corners. The space looked peaceful—but something about it felt arranged, built to resemble belonging, rather than hold it.

Kael stood just inside the door, unmoving.

That's when he saw him.

Eshan.

Flowing linen. Movements measured like dance. A voice like warm wind through tall grass.

He didn't speak loudly. He didn't need to. People leaned in. Smiled wider. Sat straighter. Laughed a little too quickly.

His words weren't wrong. That was what made it strange.

He led a meditation. Talked about inner light. Encouraged letting go, breathing deep, becoming still.

Kael watched. Listened. And something in him tensed.

Not because Eshan was wrong.

But because nothing in him rang true

Afterward, Kael lingered near the tea table. Not for the tea—just to anchor himself.

Eshan approached him like a man who knew he would be received.

"You've got a quiet energy," he said, his smile polished but distant.

"So I've been told," Kael answered.

"Stillness is sacred," Eshan nodded. "Unless it's a shield."

The line was well-placed. Polished. Almost poetic.

But Kael didn't flinch.

"Or a home," he said softly.

Their eyes locked for a moment too long.

Then Eshan smiled again—almost with approval—patted Kael's shoulder, and moved on.

A few days later, Kael was at the hospice—where he volunteered quietly most weeks. He would sit with patients who were too weak to talk.

Held their hands. Changed water. Brushed hair gently.

And just be there.

That day, the hospice was busier than usual. A local media team hovered with cameras. People whispered.

Then Kael saw him again.

Eshan.

Draped in white. His soft shawl neatly placed. He kneeled beside an elderly woman and laid a blanket over her legs just as a camera clicked.

Kael stood in the hallway, watching. The woman blinked, confused, as Eshan stood and walked away.

A nurse gently stepped in to sit beside her.

Later, near the vending machine, Kael heard him say to a coordinator:

You have to show compassion, you know? Visibility matters."

Kael said nothing. But something inside him cracked quietly.

That night, Kael returned to the garden.

Mira was on the old bench, polishing her shears and trimming small bundles of thyme.

The rosemary behind her swayed in the breeze.

Kael sat beside her, silent.

Finally, he spoke.

"What do you do," he asked, "when someone uses the language of truth… but doesn't live in it?"

Mira didn't look up.

"You let them speak," she said.

"And then?" he asked.

"You let your life speak louder."

Kael looked at his hands. "People were hanging on every word. Like moth to a flame."

Mira nodded, tying twine around a stalk of thyme.

"Everyone's drawn to light," she said. "But it takes time to know which light warms… and which one blinds."

She placed the bundle in her basket and finally met his eyes.

"The difference between truth and performance isn't in what's said. It's in what remains after the words are gone."

Kael swallowed.

"It's hard," he admitted. "Watching people be moved by something that feels like paper."

Mira's gaze softened.

“The flame doesn’t shine for applause,” she said.

“It shines because that’s what it is.”

Kael hesitated.

“There was this man—”

He described a moment from a day earlier: near the cathedral park, a man in a tattered coat had asked for directions, nervous and lost.

Eshan had scoffed and waved him off, never slowing down.

Minutes later, an elderly man walking his dog had stepped in.

No speeches. No praise.

Just a hand on the stranger’s shoulder and a quiet walk toward the bus stop.

Kael looked at Mira.

“One had the words.

The other had the flame.”

She closed her eyes briefly, as if in prayer.

“Let your eyes remember that difference.”

Later that week, Kael sat in his room, notebook open.

He stared at the page. Then finally, he wrote:

> **Eshan** — His voice is clear. Not false. Just unfinished.

He set the pen down.

The rest wasn't for the page.

Just a quiet thought rising in his chest:

I want to hear what he says when no one's listening.

I used to think anyone who spoke of light must be close to it.

But some speak because they've touched it.

And some speak because they want to be seen near it.

The flame doesn't perform.

It endures.

He closed the book and pressed it to his chest.

Outside, a dog barked.

A baby cried, then was quieted.

Laughter floated up from the street below.

Small, ordinary flames—

not asking to be seen.

Just burning, quietly, on.

Chapter 8

What Stirs in Us

Kael was twenty-two when she arrived.

It was the kind of afternoon when the light had shifted—no longer bright, not yet fading. It filtered through the trees like a memory returning, half-formed, not yet whole.

He was sitting in the courtyard behind the community library, sketching. Nothing elaborate—just the way light moved through branches. It was a habit he'd never outgrown, a way to listen to the world without words.

She sat beside him without asking.

He didn't look up at first.

"Are you drawing sunlight or sadness?"

Her voice was low, clear, unhurried—words landing like leaves on still water. Quiet. Unmistakable.

Kael glanced sideways. She wasn't watching his sketch—she was watching the light itself.

"Both," he said.

She nodded like that made perfect sense. "Thought so. You look like someone trying to translate the wind."

She introduced herself—Eirene. A name that lingered like a whisper, soft yet resonant.

When he took her hand, something in him paused. Not dramatically. Not in shock.

Just... aligned.

They kept running into each other after that.

On the back steps of the library. At the co-op. Outside a poetry reading neither of them enjoyed.

It wasn't planned.

It wasn't rushed.

But it kept happening.

And every time, something in Kael—something he'd worked hard to manage, contain, soften—rose up to meet her.

Eirene didn't speak like most people did. She didn't fill silence—she listened to it, the way Mira did.

But where Mira's silence had wrapped around him like warmth, Eirene's came with edges. She was kind, but not eager. Gentle, but not soft. Her quiet carried fire.

She asked the kind of questions no one else dared to voice.

"What's the one thing you feel and never say?" she asked once, while they walked between rows of sunlit houses.

Kael hesitated.

"Loneliness," he said.

Eirene nodded, didn't press. She just took his hand, held it like it had a right to be held.

That was how she loved.

Not loudly.

But with full attention.

They never said they were in love.

But they were—and they didn't need to name it.

It lived in the way she brought him sea salt chocolate just because he'd once said it reminded him of foggy mornings. In the way he walked three extra blocks just to catch the sound of her laugh before it disappeared into the evening.

Kael had felt needed before. But with Eirene, he felt met—seen without having to perform, chosen without having to earn it.

One night, they sat on a rooftop watching clouds shift over the city.

"You ever feel like you're meant for something," she asked, "but can't name it?"

Kael looked up at the sky. "All the time."

Eirene leaned her head against his shoulder.

"Maybe we're not meant to name it," she whispered. "Just live it."

Kael didn't answer. He didn't need to.

The moment had already answered for him.

Later that week, Kael found himself in the garden with Mira. The light was soft, catching in the rosemary.

"I met someone," he said.

Mira paused, her hands stilling in the thyme, as if she were considering the weight of his words before speaking. Her gaze lifted from the bundles of herbs, meeting his with quiet understanding. Her lips curved slightly, a knowing smile that wasn't rushed, but tempered with patience.

"And what do you feel?" she asked.

Kael hesitated.

"Like I've known her longer than time can measure."

Then listen closely—not just to her, but to what stirs within you. That's where the truth lies.

He looked at her, searching.

"But what if I want her to stay?"

She smiled, not unkindly.

"Then love her fully—and give her the freedom to stay."

She looked up then, gaze steady.

“We confuse longing with destiny sometimes,” she said. “Not everything that opens us is ours to hold. Some things bloom—and then return to seed.”

Kael walked home beneath a sky that felt too wide and too close at once.

His chest was full—not just of love, but of the terrifying, beautiful awareness that love could be real and still leave.

But it hadn’t left yet.

And tonight, that was enough.

Days passed like petals falling from a bloom—quiet, deliberate.

One evening, Eirene met him in the garden.

They sat side by side on the old bench, dusk settling soft around them. The chamomile brushed their ankles in the breeze. A folded jacket lay between them, forgotten.

“You don’t make me explain myself,” she said softly. “That’s rare.”

Kael turned to her.

“You don’t make me hide,” he whispered.

They didn’t kiss. They didn’t need to.

They simply breathed—into the silence, into each other.

And somewhere in that stillness, something in him softened.

Not because she completed him.

But because she mirrored the part he'd stopped believing was still there.

Not because they were unfinished—but because together, they remembered how to be. Gently. Honestly. Without needing to know where it would lead.

In that silence beneath the fading light of the day, everything felt whole. Nothing more was asked. Nothing more was needed.

Chapter 9
The Way Back Home

The world hadn't softened. Not really.

But something in Kael had.

Enough to notice the way light curved over peeling bricks,

or how grief moved through people's eyes

like shadows behind glass.

It wasn't clarity.

But it was something.

One almost-quiet evening, Kael saw a man no one else seemed to see.

Beneath a flickering streetlight near the old quarter, a man crouched beneath the buzzing lamp, wrapped in an oversized jacket—more hole than cloth. A crumpled paper cup sat beside him.

His beard tangled like grief grown wild.

People passed him like he was part of the sidewalk.

Kael stopped.

The man looked up; eyes sharp.

"What? You going to hand me a Holy Book? Tell me to 'keep my chin up'?"

"No," Kael said quietly. "I don't have anything to give."

"Then move along."

But Kael sat—close, but not beside him.

"You serious?" the man muttered.

"I don't know. Maybe."

The silence was jagged. Not like Mira's—hers was a hand on the back.

This one had rust. Teeth.

"You one of those feels-too-much kids?"

"Yeah," Kael said. "I guess I am."

The man gave a dry laugh. "Dangerous way to live."

"I'm learning that."

Eventually, the man muttered,

"Name's Tomás. Used to be a teacher. Before the bottle and the system ate me."

"What did you teach?"

"History. Spent twenty years telling kids how we repeat the same mistakes. And now I'm one of them."

Kael looked at him—not with pity, just presence.

"You're not a mistake."

Tomás blinked, looked away.

"Don't do that."

"Do what?"

"See me like I still matter."

Kael didn't flinch.

He just stayed.

After a while, Tomás wiped his eyes.

"Damn poets. You people ruin a good collapse."

They stayed there—two shadows beneath a fading lamp.

No saving. No sermon.

Just breath.

Kael didn't fix Tomás's life.

He simply gave back what Tomás thought he'd lost:

Dignity.

When the streetlight blinked out, Tomás grunted,

"Guess even the lights give up."

Kael stood.

"They don't give up," he said. "They rest before they shine again."

"You write that in your little poet notebook?"

Kael smiled faintly.

"Maybe."

As he turned the corner, Tomás hadn't moved—

But something in his posture had.

Just enough.

That night, Kael opened a fresh page:

Tomás — softened.

In a hospital waiting room, a woman named Amina sat alone, hands shaking around a crumpled sonogram.

Kael sat nearby. Said nothing.

After twenty minutes, she let out a bitter chuckle.

"Last time I was here, I was naming baby clothes after fruit. Peach pajamas. Banana booties."

Her voice cracked.

"I don't even like bananas."

Kael didn't smile, but he breathed deeper—matching hers.

She folded the sonogram more gently.

"I didn't think anyone could sit with this kind of sadness."

"The hardest things to carry," Kael said, "aren't meant to be carried alone."

She exhaled. Not relief—just less resistance.

And in that breath, a flicker of permission.

She didn't answer. But her hands stilled.

Her grief remained—

But it was no longer stranded.

Later, Kael passed a man curled behind a dumpster.

He offered a granola bar.

"I'm allergic to nuts, genius."

The bar bounced off Kael's chest.

He picked it up.

"Right. Sorry."

Trying to help didn't always feel helpful.

But still, he showed up.

On a slow-moving train, Kael sat across from a boy—maybe fourteen.

"Why are you looking at me?" the boy snapped.

"You seem like someone carrying something too heavy."

"My dad left. My mom says 'be strong.' But I don't know what that means."

"Sometimes being strong just means letting yourself feel it."

The boy didn't speak. But his eyes welled.

He cried—quietly.

Like a door creaking open just enough to let in light.

When Kael stepped off the train, he left more than silence.

He left a key.

To cry.

To feel.

To not be okay.

These weren't grand acts.

No crowds. No praise.

But Kael had begun to understand—

The flame did not live in spectacle.

It lived in staying.

It lived in seeing.

He still stumbled. Still doubted.

Still there were days when sorrow felt like too much.

But he no longer waited for clarity.

Sometimes, they found him.

Other times, he simply went—

to the garden,

to the co-op,

to corners where silence had grown too heavy.

He sat where others didn't.

Listened where others passed.

Waited, quietly,

until pain felt safe enough to speak.

Sometimes, the smallest light

was enough to guide someone home—

not to a place,

but to themselves,

reminding them how to begin again.

Chapter 10

The Place Where Hearts Rest

The rhythm between Kael and Eirene had begun to shift—gently, like the turn of a season.

Not the silence of peace but of searching.

They still laughed sometimes. Still shared glances that said more than words.

But the thread between them had begun to loosen—quietly, almost lovingly.

Kael noticed it first in the way Eirene's smile reached him, but didn't stay.

In the spaces between her sentences, where questions hung—half-formed and unanswered.

Fewer letters tucked into books.

Fewer impromptu conversations.

More pauses.

More distance.

One afternoon, sunlight trickled through the golden leaves of a maple as she sat beside him—legs pulled close, gaze distant.

"Kael," she said, "do you ever feel like you're being led somewhere you can't yet see?"

He nodded.

"Almost always."

She looked at him with eyes full of sorrow and love.

"I think we're on the same path," she whispered.

"But walking in opposite directions."

Kael could feel the goodbye beginning.

He didn't chase her.

He didn't hold tighter.

Some part of him—deep and flame-lit—knew she wasn't meant to stay.

They sat together again beneath the maple a few days later.

The shadows had lengthened.

The air had cooled.

Eirene's voice was steady.

"It's not you," she said. "It's not even me, really.

It's just… life is pulling me somewhere I don't yet understand."

Kael watched her hands as she spoke.

They had once felt like home.

Now, they trembled—like something sacred was loosening.

He didn't argue.

He didn't beg.

He listened.

When she stood to leave, she pressed her forehead to his, and for a moment, the ache wasn't pain.

It was reverence.

And then she was gone.

Later that week, Kael returned to the garden to find Mira tending the rosemary with slower hands.

Her shawl was pulled tighter around her shoulders.

"She's gone," he said.

"Yes," Mira replied.

They sat in silence, listening to the wind stir the leaves like memory.

"You knew she would be."

"I didn't know," Mira said softly.

"But I trusted the flame would carry what needed to come…

and release what needed to leave."

Kael closed his eyes, the ache pressing low in his chest.

The garden felt different now.

Not because it held joy—

but because it held everything.

"Love, real love," Mira said,

"doesn't keep you from the fire.

It walks you through it."

Kael didn't speak.

But her words settled deep, like water on thirsty soil.

He returned the next evening, and Mira made tea.

The cup was warm between his hands,

but his chest felt like winter.

He hadn't cried.

But the ache was there—

low and quiet, like something unfinished inside him.

Mira poured more water into the pot, her movements slow and tender.

“You know,” she said gently, “I wasn’t always alone here.”

Kael looked up.

“I had a husband. Long ago.”

He blinked.

Mira had always felt complete in her solitude—rooted.

“We were very different,” she said.

“I talked to flowers. He talked to clocks.

He liked systems. I liked soul.

He didn’t understand why I needed stillness.

I didn’t understand why he couldn’t stop moving.

We argued. We missed each other often—

in timing, in tone.

But something in us kept softening.”

Kael listened, feeling something stretch and settle in him.

“Eventually, he learned to slow down.

I learned to be clearer.

We built a rhythm. Not perfect. But real.

He anchored me. I opened him."

She looked out at the olive tree.

"He died gently. One morning.

I held his hand until the last breath.

It was quiet. Just peace."

Kael looked down.

"I thought people like you were always alone.

That the path made it... impossible."

Mira shook her head.

"The path only asks that you stay true to the flame.

It never said you had to walk it without company."

"But what if it doesn't work out?"

"Sometimes it won't," she said.

"Even when it looks perfect, something shifts.

And sometimes, when it looks impossible, the thread holds."

"Like you and him?"

"Exactly.

And sometimes," she added, "a person only walks beside you for a little while.

Like Eirene. Or Niva.

That doesn't make it a failure.

That makes it a spark."

She reached into her basket and placed a small sprig of thyme in his palm.

"This," she said, "is what letting go with gratitude smells like."

Kael breathed in.

Earthy. Bright. Slightly sweet.

He didn't cry.

But something loosened in his chest.

"How do I know who's meant to stay?"

"Time," she said.

"Time will reveal when life wants us to keep—

and when it asks us to release.

Let your love be real.

Let your heart be open.

But let the flame lead."

She leaned back in her chair, voice barely a whisper.

"Among all the achievements in life, Kael...

the greatest honor is to be a place where someone's heart has rested.

Even just for a while."

Kael closed his eyes.

And for the first time since Eirene left,

he felt... peace.

That night, he returned to the garden alone.

Mira wasn't there.

But her presence lingered in the stones,

in the wind,

in the rhythm of the rosemary.

He sat beside the cold fire pit,

watching shadows lean against the earth.

The coals were black,

but not forgotten.

And as he stared into the ash,

he placed a hand over his chest and whispered:

"I let someone see me.

And I didn't disappear."

The flame inside him stirred.

Not with heat,

but with weight.

It didn't blaze.

It settled.

Deeper than it ever had before.

And for the first time, Kael understood:

Some flames stay. Some go.

Some pass by and leave light behind.

The flame doesn't need permanence to be real.

It only asks to be received.

Love doesn't save you from the fire.

It walks you through it.

Chapter 11
The Passing of Flame

The garden had grown wilder in Kael's absence.

Vines curled freely across the harbor. Moss softened the cracked stones. Even the wind chimes sang more slowly—like they'd learned to breathe between notes.

Kael stepped through the gate like a silent offering.

The air smelled of lavender and time.

He hadn't seen Mira in weeks.

Life had pulled him outward—through heartbreak, into city streets, among strangers who left gentle imprints.

But something had begun to tug at him. A quiet knowing. A call without words.

He followed it back here.

And there, beneath the olive tree, Mira sat wrapped in a quilted shawl, her hands folded in her lap. Her body was smaller now. Her breath slower.

But her eyes still held constellations.

"You came," she said, her voice thin but warm.

"I didn't know how to stay away," Kael replied.

He knelt beside her, the missing settling in like a hush.

"I felt something," he said.

"You did," Mira said. "You felt me."

He looked at her closely, taking in the fragile grace of her face.

"How long have you known?"

She smiled faintly. "Long enough to make peace. Not long enough to stop tending the flowers."

Kael swallowed the ache rising in his throat.

"You always knew this would come," he whispered.

"Yes," she said. "And so did you. In your own way."

They sat in silence beneath the tree that had watched them both grow—Kael into himself, Mira into her final chapter.

"I've been walking," he said.

"I know," she whispered. "I've felt the air shifting around you."

"I feel like I'm supposed to help, but… half the time I just want to disappear."

She nodded gently.

"And do you know what that means?"

Kael met her eyes, burning.

"It means you're still human."

Then Mira said, "The flame doesn't spare you, Kael. It strips you. Gently, but completely."

Silence settled between them—not heavy, not sad. Just whole.

"Do you remember the first time you came here?" she asked.

"I was seven. You told me I had the eyes of an old soul."

She smiled. "And now you have the heart of one, too."

Tears found their way to the surface.

"You changed everything for me."

"I didn't change you," Mira said. "I just saw what was already there."

She leaned her head against the bark of the tree.

"And now... it's your turn to see it in others."

After a while, she took his hand. Her fingers trembled slightly.

"I have nothing more to teach you," she said. "You're not meant to be a student anymore."

"I'm afraid," he whispered.

"You won't lose me," she said. "You'll carry me."

He swallowed.

"But I'm not ready."

"No one ever is," she said.

"The flame isn't passed when you're certain—it's passed when you're true. And still, we keep it lit."

She looked toward the basil swaying in the breeze.

"This world forgets—names, faces, what it means to feel without flinching.

But you… you remember. And you help others remember."

Her voice grew faint.

"The flame isn't yours, Kael. It never was. It moves through whoever is willing to carry it.

Now… it's time."

He wanted to reach for her, to stop time.

But something in her gaze—clear and eternal—quieted the protest before it rose.

She wasn't going anywhere.

The next morning, Kael returned to the garden.

The sky was bruised with clouds, heavy with what hadn't been said.

He stood in the doorway, still as silence.

Everything looked as it always had—the rosemary, the cracked path, the bowl of water for birds.

But still, it felt different.

The air held an emptiness. A stillness that rang louder than any sound.

He sat beneath the olive tree, the weight of its shade heavy on his shoulders.

Time passed, but it felt like it had stopped.

The ache wasn't sharp. It was vast—like a sky missing one of its stars.

He shed no tears. Nothing could fill the space she left.

The notebook lay unopened.

When he finally reached for it, his hands trembled.

The words that once came easily now slipped through his fingers like water.

Then, closing it, he whispered into the air,

"You are gone.

And yet... you are everywhere."

He lowered himself to the soil and pressed his palm to the earth.

"Thank you," he said.

"For letting me belong."

Kael buried a flower at the foot of the olive tree.

He didn't mark it with stone.

He marked it with presence.

And from that day on, whenever he returned to the garden, he didn't feel alone.

Mira was there.

In the roots. In the hush.

In the soft resilience of the wind.

Kael rarely cried.

But some nights, he'd sit in the corner where the basil grew thick, and let the stars soften into light.

Once, a breeze stirred the sage, and he could almost hear her humming—that quiet, tuneless murmur she made with her hands in the soil.

He closed his eyes and let it wrap around him.

Not grief. Just remembering.

In the weeks that followed, people came to the garden more often.

Not to mourn. They hadn't known her well.

But the space had shifted.

It held something.

A kind of warmth that couldn't be named.

Kael tended it like a living memory.

He didn't speak of Mira much.

But he began to become her.

Listening deeper.

Looking longer.

Staying present—especially when it hurt.

And the flame burned differently now.

Not because she was gone.

But because she had gone into him.

One afternoon, as he trimmed the mint, someone said,

"I never talked to her much. But I always felt better when she was around."

Kael smiled faintly.

"She didn't talk much either," he said. "But she was always listening."

That evening, under the tree, Kael opened his notebook and wrote:

Some people don't teach with words.

They teach with presence.

And when they leave… their presence becomes part of you.

Mira didn't just tend the garden.

She taught me how to tend the soul.

Now the flame is mine to carry.

Not because I asked for it.

But because she gave it freely.

And so, I carry her too.

Quietly. Steadily.

As she once carried me.

Chapter 12

What Stays

Kael arrived at the co-op in the late afternoon; eyes red but dry. He didn't say a word.

Soren didn't ask. He didn't need to.

Instead, he nodded toward the back.

"Compost bin railing's loose. Was going to fix it. Come if you want."

Which was Soren's way of saying:

I heard about Mira. I know.

Kael just hung his jacket on the same old hook and followed.

They worked in silence.

The sun slanted across the floorboards.

Soren hammered. Kael held the rail.

After a while, Kael spoke—quiet, but tight.

"You act like you don't care," he said. "But you do.

You show up. You fix things. You never say it, but you care.

So why make it so hard for people to see?"

Soren paused. Sat back on his heels. Not angry—just still.

"Because saying it never did much for me," he said.

"You say it, and people still leave.

But you fix a door? Patch a wall?

Build something that stays?

That means something."

Kael didn't respond right away. But something in his chest loosened.

Soren stood, stretched his back, picked up the hammer.

"You going to help or just stand there feeling things?"

Kael smiled, faintly. "Both."

They worked side by side. No speeches. No grand healing. Just staying.

For that day—the silence, the repair—it was enough.

Some things couldn't be spoken.

They had to be lived through, tended to in the quiet.

After that day, Kael understood:

Presence was its own kind of balm.

Later that week, Kael stopped by the shelter.

He'd been coming now and then—stocking supplies, sitting with people who didn't need fixing, just company.

The place wasn't much—peeling paint, a door that stuck when it rained.

But it held.

There, Kael often crossed paths with Rowan.

A caseworker in her thirties—short curls, broad shoulders, fierce, worn thin.

She'd once believed she could change the world.

Now, she just tried to get through the day.

Her voice had the clipped sharpness of someone always bracing for something.

But when she spoke to children, it softened.

She had noticed Kael.

The way people settled near him without knowing why.

But until today, she hadn't said anything.

"You don't talk much," she said.

He shrugged.

"But people settle near you," she added. "Like they know you'll listen."

Then, sharper: "You think feeling everything makes you wise?

It doesn't.

It makes you useless.

Compassion doesn't pay rent. Love doesn't stop evil.

Kael nodded. "You're right."

She blinked, surprised.

"Love doesn't stop evil," he said. "But it survives it.

And sometimes, it undoes it—one small act at a time."

Rowan scoffed.

There was a pause.

"I used to believe that," she said.

"Until I watched a girl get sent back to the father who broke her ribs—

while the judge called him 'redeemed.'

That's when I knew better."

Kael didn't look away.

His voice stayed soft. "That's not knowing better.

That's forgetting.

Just... forgetting softer."

She didn't respond. But she didn't walk away either.

Another day, she stayed behind after helping a grieving mother fill out paperwork.

"She couldn't even look me in the eye," Rowan said.

"She didn't need you to be strong," Kael replied. "She needed you to stay."

He paused. "Some people won't know how to say what they need.

When they don't, they might sound angry or cold.

But sometimes, that's just pain without a voice."

Rowan didn't say thank you.

But she returned the next day.

And the day after that.

Over time, she began to sit with him.

First in silence. Then in questions. Then stories.

Her edges began to soften—not completely,

But enough for light to pass through.

She didn't smile.

But she didn't flinch when their hands brushed reaching for the same cup.

Not everyone woke the same way.

Some needed years. Some, entire lifetimes.

One evening, Rowan stayed late, sorting through the donation bin.

She'd done it a hundred times.

Old clothes. Worn shoes. Nothing new.

Then, tucked beneath a blanket, she found a chipped music box.

A ballerina twisted mid-spin beneath cracked glass.

It smelled of dust and forgotten things.

It hadn't worked when it was donated.

She'd never bothered trying.

But today, absentmindedly, she turned the key.

And for a moment, a soft tune played. Faint. Brief. Sweet.

Her breath caught.

She blinked.

Then, sharply, she snapped the lid shut and tucked it back into the pile.

The music had stopped.

But the sound lingered,

Just enough

To stir something inside her.

And for the first time in years,

She didn't turn away from it.

Chapter 13
The Sacred Work

One afternoon, a woman sat in the far corner of the garden, her head bowed, shoulders drawn tight as if bracing against a storm only she could feel. Kael approached quietly, the scent of rosemary rising in the warm breeze. He offered her a cup of tea, his hands steady, voice low.

She didn't look up.

"You don't have to talk," Kael said, settling beside her without crowding her space. "You're allowed to just be."

She nodded slightly, her eyes shimmering with grief too old for words.

The wind rustled the chimes, and the garden around them breathed, its sounds soft and steady.

After a long while, she whispered, "Someone hurt me. Bad. And I don't know if I'll ever be okay."

Kael didn't answer immediately. A memory rose within him—Mira, stirring her tea in that quiet, deliberate way that made time feel slower.

"You know," Mira had said years ago, "not all wounds come from losing someone you loved. Some wounds come from what should never have happened at all."

"There are people, Kael, who've been hurt in ways too deep for words. And many close themselves off, turn cold just to survive."

She paused, looking out the window as a crow glided across a gray sky.

"But some… still choose to live with an open heart. Even when it aches. Even when the world never said sorry. That kind of choice," she smiled faintly, "keeps the whole tapestry alive."

Kael had asked her once, "Where does the flame go, if no one remembers?"

Mira had been silent a long time before answering. "To the ones who still ache. The ones who survived. The ones who hurt may never open. But the ones who were hurt still can. And every time they do, it lights a piece of the pattern the others refused to carry."

She had placed her hand over Kael's chest then, warm and grounding. "That's not fair, Kael. But it's how the flame continues. The flame remembers them—even when no one else does."

The memory softened the ache pressing in his ribs. Kael turned back to the woman beside him. The garden around them exhaled—the faint smell of damp earth and sweet blossoms in the misty air.

He spoke quietly, his voice firm but gentle, "You don't have to be okay today. But you're here. And the fact that you still feel —that's the flame still burning."

Her breath caught, a small shudder rippling through her shoulders.

Kael continued, his voice steady, "Some people hold on to the pieces of what was done to them, thinking their worth was broken with it. But the flame doesn't measure by perfection. It lives in the breath. In the trying. In staying soft—even when you have every reason not to."

"You may never get an apology. You may never see justice arrive. But even in the worst pain, your soul still has a voice. You still matter. Not because of what happened to you, but because you lived through it, and you still have light to give."

The words hung between them for a moment.

"There are wounds the world can't explain. Things taken without reason, without mercy. Innocence shattered. Futures lost. And no flame should pretend that didn't happen."

He lowered his voice, "But there is a kind of justice the world can't give you. It's the justice of staying whole. It's choosing, every day, to feel what they tried to make you numb to. To cry when the world said be silent. To love again when your heart was told it should never open."

He leaned slightly forward, his words more intimate now, "If you can hold on to your softness—if you can live without becoming like the ones who hurt you—you've already done something powerful. You've protected what they tried to take."

The air seemed to still around them.

"That is sacred work," he said quietly. "Not the kind of justice that punishes them, but the kind that sets you free."

"And if you're still breathing—still soft somewhere inside—then you are the one carrying justice now."

Kael let the silence settle between them, allowing his words to sink in.

"The flame knows," he finished softly. "It always knows."

The woman cried then. Not loudly. Not tragically. Just honestly. Tears slipping through the cracks of all the places she had braced herself against feeling. Tears that did not weaken her. They made her real again.

Kael stayed with her, not trying to fix it. Only bearing witness. The way Mira had taught him. The way the flame had asked him to.

The rosemary trembled in the breeze. The jasmine swayed lightly. Somewhere unseen, another thread in the great pattern quietly caught fire—because one person, one soul, had chosen to stay soft. And that was enough.

Chapter 14
Silent Lanterns

Later that week, he helped a retired co-op member move into a quiet apartment above a ceramics shop. Narrow stairs. An alley with a crooked fence dividing the lot from an overgrown schoolyard.

He wasn't thinking about healing. Just dinner, maybe. A quiet evening.

But as he passed the alley, something caught—a flicker, a stillness.

At the far end of the fence, a woman sat hunched, face in her hands. Shoulders barely shaking. The kind of crying that's been held back too long.

Beside her—still and cross-legged—sat another woman.

No touch. No words. Just presence.

Kael stilled.

Then he saw the embroidered napkin being offered. Not a tissue. A small cloth.

His breath caught.

Niva.

She hadn't seen him. And he didn't move.

The woman didn't thank her. But after a moment, she leaned—just slightly—toward Niva.

And Niva stayed.

No catharsis. Just presence.

Something stirred in him. Ache. Wonder.

He had once sat across from Niva, aching to be met. She hadn't been ready. That had hurt.

Still, he hadn't pushed. He stayed. Without pressure, without demand.

And that patience had become something living in her.

Now, she was the one staying.

This, he understood, was what it meant to hold space. Not forever. Not perfectly. Just long enough for someone to grow into themselves.

The warmth rising in his chest wasn't pride. It was older. Deeper. Familiar.

Someone had done the same for him once.

He saw it now—not just in memory, but in truth.

A cracked hand on his forehead. Bread warm from the oven. No speeches. Just presence.

His mother.

She hadn't always understood him. But she protected his softness anyway. With quiet survival. With staying.

And that, he realized, had been sacred.

He turned from the alley—not out of pain, but peace. Something inside had shifted.

Not every goodbye is a wound. Some people grow after you part. And sometimes, the most loving thing is to let them.

That night, Kael wrote:

Some threads don't need to be completed—just honored. Some flames carry our intent onward. Another hand picks up where we had to let go.

Maybe the flame knows how to stitch things forward—if we stay open enough to let it.

"Mira helped me remember who I am," he whispered. "But my mother… she held me in the world long enough to find her."

That evening, he brought tea to his mother's door.

They hadn't spoken in a while. Life had moved outward—for both of them.

She opened the door before he could knock.

"Kael," she said, like a breath she hadn't known she was holding.

Inside, the apartment was warm and small. A cinnamon candle flickered. She set out two mugs while he unpacked the tea.

They sat at the table. Steam curled between them.

"You were always a strange child," she said with a small smile. "Too tender for this world."

"I used to think that meant something was wrong with me."

She looked down. "I was scared your softness would be broken. I didn't know how to meet it."

He reached for her hand. "You stayed," he said. "And that's more than enough."

Her eyes welled, but she didn't look away.

"I see it now—the light in you. I just didn't know how to hold it."

"You held it anyway," he said.

Their hands stayed folded between them. No more defenses. Just presence.

Kael had stopped offering answers. Stopped reaching too quickly for meaning. He just listened. Stayed.

And he noticed things.

The elderly woman who folded every flyer four times before setting it down.

The boy who flinched when praised.

The girl who never asked for water—but always brought it.

The woman who apologized whenever she took up space.

The teenager who asked about volunteer work but couldn't meet his gaze.

They held silences, not just stories.

In each, he saw a flicker of Niva—not in the details, but in the courage to stay soft in a world that asked them to harden.

She had been the first flame.

But now he saw: she was never alone.

The flame lived in others too.

Low-burning. Hearth-like. Quiet but steady.

Burning in the eyes of a midwife whispering prayers to newborns, or in a man holding his daughter's hand as if the touch itself were a prayer.

It warmed the silence of a man who sat beside his neighbor, listening and laughing like it were the first time.

The flame passed soul to soul—no spotlight. No grand gesture.

Just presence.

Each heart, a lantern.

Each act of tenderness, a star.

This wasn't noise. It was liturgy.

A sacred rhythm disguised as daily life.

Kael watched. Listened. Sometimes smiled.

He no longer felt the need to be the fire.

His hands rested on the table, warm against the wood.

In that quiet, he felt it:

The flame within him.

Finally still.

He closed his eyes and whispered:

"Wherever someone chooses love over fear,

truth over silence,

presence over numbness—

Heaven enters the room.

Not above, but here.

Now. Reflected in this very moment."

Chapter 15

The Great Remembering

Kael knew his time was near.

Not through pain or prophecy—

the silence had changed.

No longer waiting,

but watching.

Not holding breath,

but bearing witness.

As if Heaven itself had opened its eyes—

not to call him home,

but to welcome him back.

One evening, Kael returned to Mira's Garden—now tended by hands he had once guided.

Children laughed as they chased the wind through the tall grass.

Flowers bloomed in wild, defiant beauty.

The garden hadn't changed much.

The olive tree still leaned slightly east, toward the rising sun.

The chimes still moved like breath across memory.

And the path still curved gently, as if it had always been leading him back here.

Kael stepped through the gate with slow reverence.

He was older now—not in years, but in knowing.

The kind that settles not in the mind, but in the bones.

He didn't come to say goodbye.

He came to remember.

He sat beneath the olive tree, where Mira had once told him the flame would grow.

He looked at his hands.

At the calluses and scars.

At all the ways he had been touched—and all the ways he had touched others.

Kael closed his eyes.

The silence deepened.

And then… the Voice.

Not sudden.

Not loud.

Like leaves rustling in sacred rhythm.

"You have returned."

"I never truly left," he answered.

"And now you see the full thread."

They came not as flashes, but as warmth moving through bone and breath.

Mira's steady hands.

Eirene's eyes, soft with mercy.

Soren's unshakable loyalty.

Niva's laughter, bright as the wind.

Rowan's quiet strength.

And then—faces he didn't recognize.

Souls he had never met.

Flames, lit by flames, lit by flames—

each spark passing on what could not be held.

All of it... connected.

"Then my life... was part of it all?"

"Every ache.

Every pause.

Every time you loved when it hurt—

you brought Heaven closer."

Kael breathed deeply, and the wind joined him.

"I was tested."

"Yes," said the Voice.

"Not to prove yourself worthy—

but to show yourself true.

To burn through joy and grief alike.

To hold the flame, even when the world offered you a way out."

He placed his hand over his chest.

The ember—now a flame—was there.

Warm.

Alive.

Brighter than it had ever been.

"So the test was never about passing."

"No," the Voice whispered.

"It was about choosing—

to remember what you are.

And to help others do the same."

Kael looked to the sky.

And for the first time, he didn't feel torn between here and there.

He saw no line between Earth and Heaven—

only a tapestry.

Golden threads, shining between lives.

They moved with warmth, like breath woven through stars.

And some...

Some hung cold.

Still connected. But unmoving.

Not cut. Not broken. Just... untouched.

He knew then:

Not everyone chooses to burn.

Some live their whole lives

untouched by the flame.

Not because it wasn't offered—

but because they turned away

too many times.

there was no thread left to carry them home.

And when the time came—when their breath ceased and their names faded from the world—

they did not rise.

They remained in silence.

Not as punishment.

But as consequence.

And they saw—

The luminous ones, floating free—

those who had suffered, and still stayed soft.

Who loved, forgave,

and walked the hard road with light in their hands.

And the cold ones wept.

Not because they were banished.

But because they had banished themselves.

Even those who refuse to feel cannot escape pain.

There is no protection from the truth of our choices.

Kael felt it in his chest—like something loosening, something breaking open.

He saw lives threaded with quiet courage.

Hands that healed without being asked.

Spirits that forgave without ever hearing "I'm sorry."

Souls who stayed soft, even when the world gave them every reason to harden.

Those who spoke truth when silence would've been safer.

Those who rose each day with grief in their bones, and still chose to give.

This was the fire.

Not the absence of pain—but the choice to stay awake inside it.

The shared, sacred refusal to turn away.

And then he knew:

Liberation isn't given. It's earned—

through presence, through openness,

through the sacred struggle

to remain kind in a world that tries to close you.

Those who burn become weightless.

Those who turn away become heavy.

And love—

Love keeps the count.

A shimmer passed through the garden.

The air turned golden.

From within the golden light came Mira—not as she was, but as she had always been.

Her voice, gentle as moonlight:

“The flame never forced you, Kael.

And you never forced it.

You let it burn slowly.

You let it teach you through staying.

You didn’t demand answers before their time.

You trusted the warmth to guide you.

That was always enough.

You made the garden larger, Kael.

Not with walls, but with welcome."

And beside her, the Voice— warm and vast returned.

"You are ready.

Not because you are perfect—

but because you are whole.

Come home."

Kael lay back beneath the olive tree and closed his eyes.

Not in surrender.

In completion.

His passing was not loud.

No sermon. No song.

Only a soft smile—

and a breath that returned to the stars.

Chapter 16

The Flame Continues

In the garden, something bloomed—

a single flower, small and defiant, rising through a crack in the path.

And in the wind,

if one listened closely,

a voice:

"Remember."

And some did.

The ones who were open to the flame—

Not perfect.

Not fearless.

But willing.

Willing to stay.

To soften.

To begin again.

Tomás—grizzled, wounded, sharp-tongued Tomás—

began showing up every Thursday at the community kitchen,

washing dishes and sweeping floors.

"I'm not a saint," he grumbled.

"But someone sat beside me when I was a ghost.

The least I can do is be a little more human."

The other volunteers didn't know what changed him.

But they knew the kitchen felt warmer when he was there.

The woman in the hospital—Amina—

began volunteering in the hospice wing.

She didn't have training.

She just sat with the dying,

held their hands,

and hummed songs her grandmother used to sing.

"They don't always need answers," she said.

"Just someone who won't look away."

Rowan stayed at the shelter.

She began leaving little notes behind for others—unsigned, but full of fierce kindness.

The boy on the train grew up

and became a counselor for children who had been silenced.

These were not miracles of thunder.

No signs in the sky.

No stories written in stars.

Just people—

choosing to burn gently

in the middle of the world's noise.

Kael never asked anyone to follow him.

He never called people students.

He never spoke from a stage.

He simply stayed near the flame—his own, and others'.

And without trying to,

he lit hearts.

The garden continued to bloom,

and no one could say exactly why—

but things just grew better there.

And the notebook Kael once carried?

It was found on a bench beneath the olive tree,

pages worn soft by time and weather.

Some entries were finished—clean, whole, almost luminous.

Others were fragments.

Sentences cut off mid-thought.

Words crossed out.

Someone picked it up once,

read a few lines,

and quietly set it back down—

not out of disinterest,

but quiet respect.

Because they understood something:

Some books are not meant to be finished.

Some stories don't end in certainty or conclusion.

They continue.

And that is the point.

We close the book knowing this—

it is still being written,

living on in the hearts it stirs,

in the lives it quietly changes.

You've known someone like Kael.

You might not have had a name for them then.

They didn't speak loudly or shine in obvious ways—

but their presence lingered.

Their stillness softened something in you.

Their kindness—quiet, unassuming—gave you room to breathe.

And maybe, without knowing it,

you've been that someone too.

You stayed when it was easier to go.

You listened when silence felt safer.

And somehow, even in your weariness,

you reached for love.

That, too, is the flame.

Maybe you had someone like Kael's mother—

someone who loved fiercely

but didn't always have the words,

or the strength to speak them aloud.

Or maybe you were her—

doing your best in the noise,

carrying love in your hands

even when your voice trembled.

If you've ever felt invisible in your softness—

if the world told you to harden,

to armor up,

to be more,

be louder,

be less—

know this:

Your softness is not weakness.

It's strength.

It takes courage to remain open

in a world that begs you to close.

Maybe you knew a Mira—

someone who saw you not for who you performed,

but for who you were when the mask fell away.

Someone who waited with you through the quiet.

Let every quiet kind of love be honored—

especially the kind that stayed.

You may have carried grief no one saw.

A pain without language.

A wound that didn't scar, but shaped you.

You don't need to explain it.

You don't have to forgive it.

You don't need to make it beautiful.

But know this—

You are not apart from the sacred.

You are the sacred.

The thread and the weaver.

The light and the lantern.

The flame lives in the smallest moments:

In the breath you take in the middle of the mess.

In the truth that cracks your voice.

In the tears you don't hide.

In the stillness you give someone else to feel seen.

It burns in the choice to be kind—again.

To begin—again.

To remain—again.

Now that you've walked with Kael—

if tomorrow feels too heavy,

if the world spins too fast,

if hope feels lost behind you—

Pause.

Place your hand over your heart.

Breathe.

Feel that ember.

It was never anyone else's gift.

It's been yours all along.

Let your life be a doorway.

Let your presence be a soft gate.

And when someone comes to you—uncertain, hurting, afraid—

may they feel, in your presence,

what they've longed to believe:

They are not forgotten.

They are not alone.

Heaven does not wait far above, or far ahead—

It blooms right here:

in this breath,

in this choice,

in this sacred, flawed, human heart.

The flame continues.

And now—

it lives in you.

Not the end.

Not really.

Just maybe—

the beginning.

About the Author

Dr. Faris Basheer is a debut author drawn to stories that speak softly but stay with you. The Soul's Touch: A Quiet Journey into Awakening and Healing is his first novel—a deeply personal exploration of memory, truth, and quiet transformation.

Though he doesn't come from a traditional literary background, his writing is shaped by years of deep listening—to silence, sorrow, beauty, and to people who carry quiet strength. Much of his inspiration comes from the unseen moments that are often overlooked—yet carry us through.

He believes the most powerful truths come not from preaching, but from presence. If this story can be a gentle companion to someone in the dark—or help even one reader feel a little less alone—then it has done what it was meant to do.

He lives in Kerala, India, where he continues to write stories that hold space for stillness, tenderness, and the sacredness of becoming.

You may write to the author at: drfarisbasheer@gmail.com

He is deeply grateful to every reader who has shared in this journey. May these pages help you remember the light still flickering within.

Acknowledgments

This book was not written alone.

To my wife—your unwavering presence, gentle strength, and quiet faith in this journey have been the heartbeat behind it all. Thank you for walking beside me, flame in hand.

To those who listened when I doubted, believed when I faltered, and held the flame beside me when I couldn't hold it myself—thank you.

To the ones who live quiet, honest lives and love deeply without being seen—this story carries your spirit.

To the stories that came before mine, and to the silence that shaped the words—thank you.

And to you, dear reader—whether you arrived in stillness or searching, may this book meet you gently where you are.

With deep reverence,

Dr. Faris B. M.

www.ingramcontent.com/pod-product-compliance
Lightning Source LLC
Chambersburg PA
CBHW011803160726
48282CB00035B/1242
9789334308211